W9-DGC-548

Royal Princess Academy

DRAGON DREAMS

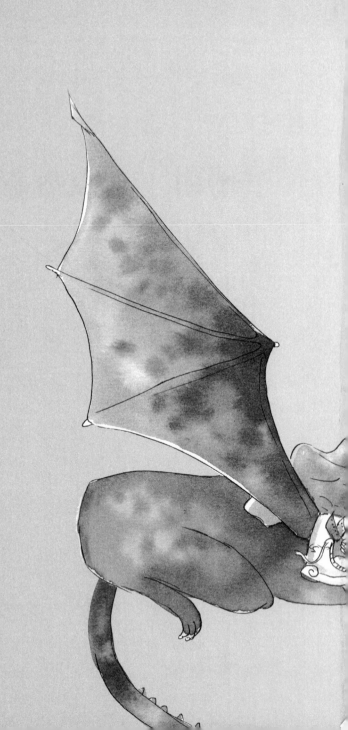

Royal Princess Academy

DRAGON DREAMS

LAURA JOY
RENNERT

illustrated by
MELANIE
FLORIAN

 Dial Books for Young Readers
an imprint of Penguin Group (USA) Inc.

DIAL BOOKS FOR YOUNG READERS

An imprint of Penguin Group (USA) Inc.

Published by The Penguin Group

Penguin Group (USA) Inc., 375 Hudson Street, New York, NY 10014, U.S.A.

Penguin Group (Canada), 90 Eglinton Avenue East, Suite 700, Toronto,

Ontario, Canada M4P 2Y3 (a division of Pearson Penguin Canada Inc.)

Penguin Books Ltd, 80 Strand, London WC2R 0RL, England

Penguin Ireland, 25 St. Stephen's Green, Dublin 2, Ireland

(a division of Penguin Books Ltd)

Penguin Group (Australia), 250 Camberwell Road, Camberwell,

Victoria 3124, Australia (a division of Pearson Australia Group Pty Ltd)

Penguin Books India Pvt Ltd, 11 Community Centre,

Panchsheel Park, New Delhi—110 017, India

Penguin Group (NZ), 67 Apollo Drive, Rosedale, Auckland 0632,

New Zealand (a division of Pearson New Zealand Ltd)

Penguin Books (South Africa) (Pty) Ltd, 24 Sturdee Avenue,

Rosebank, Johannesburg 2196, South Africa

Penguin Books Ltd, Registered Offices:

80 Strand, London WC2R 0RL, England

Designed by Irene Vandervoort and Mina Chung • Text set in Goudy Oldstyle

Printed in the U.S.A.

1 3 5 7 9 10 8 6 4 2

Library of Congress Cataloging-in-Publication Data

Rennert, Laura.

Dragon dreams / Laura Joy Rennert ; illustrated by Melanie Florian.

p.   cm. — (Royal Princess Academy)

Summary: Attending her first year at the Royal Princess Academy, Emma prefers soccer to ballroom
dancing and dreams of one day riding a dragon.

ISBN 978-0-8037-3750-1 (hardcover)

[1. Princesses—Fiction. 2. Individuality—Fiction. 3. Sex role—Fiction. 4. Dragons—Fiction.
5. Schools—Fiction.] I. Florian, Melanie, ill. II. Title.

PZ7.R2903Dr 2012

[E]—dc23

2012002851

To my darling Emma, her Chihuahua sidekick Lola, and her terrific group of princess friends. You're my inspiration! And no, Emma, we CAN'T get a dragon!!—L.J.R.

Contents

Royal Princess Academy

DRAGON DREAMS

~ ◎ Chapter 1 ◎ ~
All About Me

I'm Princess Emma and I'm in my first year at the Royal Princess Academy.

Yes, even princesses need to go to school. My great-grandmother, my grandmother, my mother, and all my aunts and cousins have gone to the Royal Academy. It's a family tradition.

My best friend Rapunzel and I are in the

same class. But, unlike Rapunzel, I am NOT your typical princess.

I don't like pink.

I'm too clumsy to dance.

I'm always tearing my gowns.

Here are the things I like best:

1. Kicking a soccer ball.

There is nothing better than feeling my foot connect with the ball for a shot on goal.

2. Playing with my pug and my Chihuahua.

I think *every* princess needs a dog, or two!

3. Racing my cousin Prince Ben.

I'm pretty fast, so it's always a close contest, and we both like to win.

4. Reading about magical animals.

I'm especially interested in dragons. I wish I could visit the Dragon Caverns.

5. Sliding down the castle banisters.

(Don't tell my mother, the queen!)

Our castle has lots of them and, since I'm sometimes late in the morning, this is fun AND a good way to get to breakfast on time.

We just had school picture day at the Academy. I forgot to tell my mom it was coming up. Let's just say that my picture did *not* look like any of the others. I think you'll be able to tell what I mean.

~ ◎ Chapter 2 ◎ ~
Princess Problems

NOW the most important day of the whole year—the All-School Princess Contest—is almost here. I'm a little worried about it. You see, the girls in my family have always outdone themselves in the contest. The gallery in our castle is filled with their awards. With the help of her forest friends, my great-great-grandmother Snow White led her class to victory the year the contests started. My grandmother Beauty helped her class win by sleeping the most daintily. My cousins the twelve princesses have all won trophies for dancing.

I don't think *I'm* going to win any trophies, though. Everyone's always giving me advice on how to be a proper princess.

My mother, the queen, says, "Shhh! Don't talk so loudly. A princess is as a princess does."

When I ask if I can stay up late to watch *Magical Animal Kingdom*, my grandmother Beauty says, "A princess needs her sleep."

My regal father says, "Walk, don't run. Even when she is not wearing a crown, a princess feels its weight."

It hasn't been going so well at school

either. Let's just say I'm not exactly the star student in Princess Posture class.

Can I help it if I'd rather read a book than wear it?

When we sign up for school activities, most of the other princesses decide on Royal Song and Dance. A few choose harp lessons. Some want to learn how to weave lace so fine it fits in a nutshell, and the class on Princess Party Planning is popular. I am the only princess who wants to learn about dragon care. In all of Academy history.

At our class on Royal Table Manners, not only do I not remember which fork and spoon to use, I accidentally spill the pepper, and it tickles my nose. When I sneeze, I sort of bump into my water goblet. So Moriah jumps out of the way. And sort of bumps into Alex's water goblet.

And, well, Madame is not too happy. Neither is Moriah.

Rapunzel thought it would be a good

idea for us to try out for the Royal Talent Show together. It wasn't. She was sick the day of the show! After my solo, Princess Jordan joked that they must have heard me in the neighboring kingdom.

Plus, at our first-year sleepover, all the other princesses changed into their frilly nightgowns and beribboned slippers. I changed into my *fuzzy pajamas* . . . and my *dragon slippers*.

But Royal Ball class was the biggest problem of all. I TRIED to tell my teacher I'm good at *soccer*, not dancing. She didn't believe me. Now she does.

Dear Royal Highnesses,

   After 5 pairs parting and dance instructors darting, 4 pages giggling, 3 trays a-tumbling, 2 gasping guests, and a poodle in a potted tree, we have come to the conclusion that Princess Emma might benefit from some extra dancing practice at home . . .

   Sincerely,
   Academy Headmistress Melinda

This morning, while we wait for our school assembly to start, I pass Rapunzel a note:

Do you think I'm the worst princess in the world?

Rapunzel writes back:

No. And don't say that about my best friend!

Sigh. Even her handwriting is more princess-y than mine. As I smile at her, I can't help wondering how she manages to look so perfect with our poofy school uniform *and* all that hair piled on top of her head.

~ ☺ Chapter 3 ☺ ~
Uh-Oh

"Princesses, we are expecting some visitors," says our teacher Lady Mary.

The trumpets sound. This means the Royal Guard has arrived. I wish I could go to the window to see if there are any dragons with them! We used to see dragons more frequently when I was little, but now seeing them is rare. Because dragon fire sometimes accidentally damaged forests and farms, the Royal Council limited where and when dragons could fly. So it's an extra-special treat to see them!

A Royal Herald marches into our class-room in great state. He announces: "Hear ye, hear ye. The Royal Academy's All-School Princess Contest will take place tomorrow, with each class flying its colors and banner from the castle battlements."

I have a sinking feeling. As soon as the herald and trumpeters leave, everyone starts to talk at once . . . everyone except me, that is. I feel sick to my stomach. What if I trip during the royal parade out onto the field? Or accidentally break a glass slipper! What if I do everything wrong?

As if things aren't already bad enough,

Lady Mary tells us that this year boys from the Royal Prince Academy are also going to come and help out. Great. Now *more* people will see me mess up!

Even the thought that the Royal Dragon Guard will be at the contest as a part of our Academy's tradition can't cheer me up.

"I'm no good at this stuff," I groan to Rapunzel.

"You're good at lots of things!" she tells me. "We just have to figure out the princess things you do well."

Princess Alex and Princess Moriah walk by right then. Alex says just loud enough for me to hear, "And you'd better do it fast, or our class will take last place!"

I spend the rest of the day trying to think

of princess things I might be good at. By the end of the day, my list isn't very long. At all!

Rapunzel has a plan, though. She meets me in the courtyard after the final bell, and I can see she's excited about something. She's got Princess Laura in tow.

"I've got it! You can both come home with me this afternoon and we can set up some princess events so you have some practice before the contest, Emma."

When we get to her house, she and Laura set things up.

And…I mismatch *all* the ballroom gowns and shoes, dismount from the royal carriage right in a huge mud puddle, curtsy on Laura's gown by mistake, and ride a horse like a boy with my school uniform all hiked up, when I should have been riding sidesaddle like a princess.

Afterward Rapunzel says, "Well, at least you tried. It wasn't *so* bad really."

Sigh. I wish I could ride a dragon instead! Dragon riders DON'T have to ride sidesaddle.

~ ◎ **Chapter 4** ◎ ~
# Let the
# Contest Begin

The next morning, I try to convince my mother I'm too sick to go to school. For *some reason*, she doesn't believe me.

I plan to get to the royal carriage stop late. But my cousin Ben, who goes to the Royal Prince Academy and waits at the same carriage stop, challenges me to a race. I couldn't just let him win, could I?!

Before I know it I'm at school, the trumpets are sounding, and the contest is starting. I look around for Rapunzel. She runs up to me smiling. Am I ever surprised! She whispers, "I got a haircut . . . because I like your short hair." I grin back. Rapunzel always makes me feel better.

Overhead, the Royal Dragon Guard swoops, and everyone claps. I can't take my eyes off them! The dragons sparkle in the sun as they fly, and the riders are so daring.

I hear some whispering. Moriah, Laura, and some of the other princesses have their heads together. I turn to see what they are looking at, and it's a small group of gnomes—the dragons' trainers. Wow!

I wonder if I can get close enough to ask some questions about the dragons. We don't see gnomes much these days. They are the dragon experts, and they're not out in the kingdom anymore now that the dragons can't fly freely.

"Come on, Emma!" says Rapunzel.

I've been so busy looking at the dragons, I forgot about the contests. The music starts, signaling our walk onto the field. Rapunzel gives my hand a squeeze.

The first competition is the Royal Bake-Off. The judges announce that this is a test to see who can make the lightest cake. Princess Sarah's cake is so lacy it melts on the judges' tongues. Princess Jordan's cake has pink swirls, pink polka dots, pink curlicues, *and* pink petals. It's so light it floats

right up into the air. Our classmates are cheering.

Gulp. It's my turn. My cake isn't exactly light, but it's chocolate—a chocolate volcano. Who wouldn't love that? Only

problem is, it erupts at the wrong time—
right when the judge starts to cut it! Oops!

Rapunzel wipes the sauce off her face
and licks her finger. "Yum!" she says.
"Hot fudge!"

Oh, well. I may not have won, but everyone went back for second helpings.

The next event is the "sleeping lightly" test. Princess Laura tosses and turns. The judge checks and finds a pea under her ten mattresses. Points for us! Princess Jordan can't get comfortable either. There's a jelly bean under her mattresses.

When I reach the top of my mattress pile, I'm starting to think this event will be an easy win for us. I'm too keyed up about the contest to sleep.

I sink into the softness. Mmm . . . this feels good. . . .

"Think of something that will keep you awake!" Princess Alex yells up at me. I think about my friend Bo Peep and her . . . Oh, no! . . . sheep . . . zzᵤᵤ z z zZZZZZ.

No points for me. Not only did I fall
asleep and NOT feel the rocks under my
mattresses—I didn't even wake up when I
fell off.

— ◎ Chapter 5 ◎ —
Woof!

At last it's time for an event I might have a chance of doing okay in: the Academy's Royal Dog Show.

Princess Jordan prances past with her fluffy poodle . . . which looks just like a furry puffball to me, but the judges give her a seven.

Princess Moriah poses with her dainty whippet, and Princess Laura sweeps by with her glossy afghan. The judges look impressed and give them each a score of eight.

Then Princess Alex glides past with her sleek greyhound. The crowd oohs and ahhs. She gets a perfect ten!

It's almost my turn. Which of my dogs should I enter? I bend down to pet my pug

Harold and my Chihuahua Lola. Harold smiles at me with his googly eyes. I look at the other dogs and I look at Harold. Um . . . maybe not. I'll take Lola. She's really tiny. She's got a smooth coat and short fur. She's perfect! Whew.

Except I forget one important thing . . . Lola thinks big dogs—which is *every* dog

compared to a Chihuahua—are furry monsters. We walk into the ring, and Lola becomes a Mexican jumping bean!

No points for me again. Plus it takes Princess Laura and me—*and* two judges—to catch Lola.

My team is in trouble, and it's all my fault. There's only one test left. The judges announce the True Princess Contest. It's the most important and the hardest! Each of us will be called forward to choose a card with a challenging princess problem on it. Then we have to figure out a way to solve the problem. The princes from our brother academy are going to help out.

I bite my lip. I'm so nervous, I don't think I'll be able to pick a card. "I can do this," I say to no one in particular, but I don't sound all that convincing.

Princess Jordan just picked her card. At her feet, Prince Collin kneels with the glass slipper. I look at the dainty shoe. Boy, would I rather wear high-tops! The slipper sparkles in the light. The sun glints off it, right into Princess Jordan's eyes. She's going to *step* on the glass slipper. We all gasp.

I whip my favorite rock star sunglasses out of my pocket and pass them to her.

Whew! That was close. As she slips her foot
into the shoe, Princess Jordan smiles at me.

Rapunzel picks "trapped in a tower." We
hold our breath. She's afraid of heights!

Plus, with her new short hair, she's stuck! I try to climb the tower to help her, but the walls are too smooth. Just when I get a little ways up, I start to slip back down. Princess Sarah gives me a push, but I still can't get high enough. Time is running out.

I see Princess Moriah starting her turn. The judge hands her a frog. Moriah squeezes her eyes shut.

Smooch.

Nothing happens . . .

She closes her eyes again.

SMOOCH.

The frog stays green and Moriah starts to turn red.

Things get even worse. Rapunzel's still trapped, Moriah's not having any luck with the frog, and Princess Alex just fell for the

oldest trick in the spell book: She pricked
her finger on a spinning wheel! I run around
looking for a prince to wake her with a kiss,
but suddenly they're all busy doing something else. *Boys!*

~ ◎ Chapter 6 ◎ ~
Saved by the Ball!

Lady Mary says it's my turn. I feel like I can't move. I pick a card from the choices the judges hold out to me. Oh, no! My task is to "create a happy ending." I'm totally the wrong princess for this job. What am I going to do?

I look up at Rapunzel. From the tower window she gives me a thumbs-up and calls, "You can do it!" Jordan and Laura cross their fingers for me. Moriah kisses her frog again. She mouths the word "HELP!" They're all depending on me.

Suddenly, I have an idea. I leapfrog over Moriah's frog. Jordan and Laura see what I'm doing and join in. Moriah's frog gets the idea and hops over us, and hops and hops and hops . . . away! He didn't turn into a prince, but at least he disappeared.

With all the hopping, no one sees me bend down to let Harold off his leash. I point to Princess Alex and give Harold a command. He makes a beeline for the spinning wheel as soon as he's off the leash. He leaps up and starts licking Alex's face.

Alex yawns and stretches, rubbing her eyes. Harold's definitely not a prince, but I guess a kiss is a kiss!

Even though she's still trapped in the tower, Rapunzel is so excited, she's jumping up and down. How can I rescue her? *What can I do?!*

Just then, my cousin Ben walks by. "Ben, can I borrow your ball?" I shout.

"Sure," he says, and tosses it to me.

I put the ball on the ground and take a deep breath. I concentrate on the tower. I imagine a giant bull's-eye about two-thirds of the way up. Then I kick the ball with all my might, aiming right at that target.

CLUNK.

The tower starts to teeter. Then it totters. Teeter. Totter. Teeter.

It sways all the way to the ground, and Rapunzel steps out.

I guess all those soccer practice shots paid off! I'm so happy, I do a victory dance. When I realize what I'm doing, I'm a little

surprised. I'm *dancing*, and . . . I didn't knock anything over, not by accident anyway, or bump into anybody. I think the headmistress is a little surprised too. My dance instructor beams and nods. Rapunzel runs over and gives me a huge hug.

I hear cheering and look around to see who is winning. My classmates are actually cheering for *me*! We won the contest!

Princess Laura asks if I'd share my recipe for volcano cake.

"Can we walk our dogs together one day after school?" Princess Alex asks.

The judges congratulate me. Even Prince Ben shakes my hand. "Wanna race again on the way home?" he asks. Who knows, this time I might even give him a head start. Well, maybe . . .

As we get in line to go back to our classes, the Academy librarian smiles at me. She says, "Maybe times have changed, and it's time princesses change with them."

"Hmm," I say, thinking.

"And don't give up on that dragon class." She winks. "You never know . . ."

I grin back.

When I get home, I find out Mom and Dad have invited all of our royal relatives to dinner to celebrate my class's victory. Hamburgers and s'mores!!!! Yum—my favorites! I show off our trophy, Rapunzel's Leaning Tower, and my father places it in the family gallery, on its own stand.

~ ◎ Chapter 7 ◎ ~
Dragon Dreams

Well, it's been six weeks, and I still haven't had any luck with the dragon class, but now I have a different plan. My birthday is in only four days. (I can't wait!) And I've finally decided what I want for a birthday present: a pet dragon.

Here are some of the reasons I want a dragon:

1. I love reading dragon stories and adventures.

2. Sometimes in class at the Academy, I feel so cooped up. Imagine soaring on the back of a dragon.

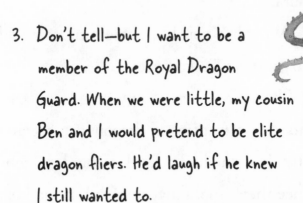

3. Don't tell—but I want to be a member of the Royal Dragon Guard. When we were little, my cousin Ben and I would pretend to be elite dragon fliers. He'd laugh if he knew I still wanted to.

4. If I have my own dragon, then I can secretly practice flying until I get good.

Unfortunately, I made the mistake of mentioning my wish for a pet dragon at school. I normally would have known better than to say anything, but I got so excited when I found out that we have a field trip to the Dragon Caverns coming up.

"Whoever heard of a princess with a pet dragon?!" said Moriah.

"Aren't you afraid of dragons?" said Laura.

"Wouldn't you like something soft and furry instead?" asked Alex.

I haven't really said anything to my parents about wanting a dragon yet because I think it might be kind of hard to convince them, too. I love my Chihuahua Lola and my pug Harold and I help take care of them, but I'm not sure my parents will believe I can take good care of a dragon.

But it's more than this. Like my friends said, princesses just don't have pet dragons. Princesses have pets that are feathery, furry, and fluffy—not pets that have hard scales, big wings, and breathe fire.

I need to find a way to prove to my parents it would be good to have a dragon for a pet and also show them I'm responsible enough to take care of a dragon.

Yikes, I'm almost late for school—too much dragon-dreaming. Ahead of me, I see Princess Laura and Princess Alex crossing the Royal Academy courtyard. "Laura, Alex! Wait for me."

"Princess Emma!" says Headmistress Melinda. "A princess shouldn't really . . . "

CRASH!

" . . . run."

Oops!

Naturally, right then, Princess Moriah
and Princess Jordan walk by. Moriah giggles
and says, "Hi, Emma. I think you need a
fairy godmother more than a pet dragon."

"Or maybe a team of fairy godmothers,"
says Jordan.

Sigh.

~ ◎ Chapter 8 ◎ ~

I Definitely Need a Plan

On my way to class, I pause to look out of one of the Academy towers. I'd like to do a dragon loop de loop in the sky! I bet it would feel amazing to see the hills and forests rushing by and to hear the whoosh of dragon wings.

Since I'm almost late for class, Rapunzel and I don't have time to talk. So, while we're working on our journals, I write her a note.

Dear Rapunzel,

Can you come over after school today and help me come up with reasons that will convince my Royal Parents we should get a pet dragon? Here's my list so far:

1. Even if I miss the carriage to school, I'll never be late again. Dragon express!
2. A dragon can help light the castle's 20 fireplaces in the winter. In almost no time!
3. With a dragon around, we'll always be able to reach the top shelves in the royal library.
4. ?

When I try to pass Rapunzel the note, she turns around and her hair knocks it onto the floor. (Poor Rapunzel! Her short haircut didn't last. Long hair runs in the family—and her hair grows fast.)

Poor *me*! Moriah sees the note before Rapunzel can get to it. She snickers. My face gets hot. Worse yet, our teacher Lady Mary picks it up. Oh no!

She smiles at me and says, "Dragons are fascinating creatures, Emma, but this isn't the time to discuss their merits as pets."

Now everyone, not just Moriah, knows I am the most un-princess-y princess in the world!

Rapunzel mouths "I'm sorry."

Luckily, Lady Mary starts talking about our upcoming field trip to the Dragon Caverns, and when we get out of class, everyone is talking about the field trip and not my note.

"I'm kind of scared of the dragons," says Alex.

"I know," says Laura. "And my father says the gnomes who live in the caverns are *really* unfriendly."

"I bet they don't want us to visit," says Moriah.

"I've never met a gnome," I say. "I wonder what they're like."

"Well, I'm excited to go to the caverns," says Rapunzel. I'm glad she says so, because after the note incident, I don't really want to admit that I'm super-excited about the field trip.

During Library, we have choice time. Alex reads stories about famous fairies who granted princesses' wishes. Jordan looks at magazines with the newest ball-gown fashions.

The Academy librarian helps me find the section on dragons. Then Rapunzel helps me cart some big books about dragons over to a corner.

Thump. Dust flies up. I guess no one has looked at these books in a while.

I use my library card to check some out.

Back at my house, Rapunzel and I decide to walk around the castle to see if we can come up with ways to make my parents think that getting a pet dragon is *their* idea. We redo my room with a dragon theme. But when my mother comes in, she says, "I love

the new decorations, girls! Maybe you can help me decorate for the upcoming ball."

Ugh. That definitely didn't go as planned.

Next, we brush our hair in front of my bedroom mirror because Rapunzel thinks this might help us come up with better ideas. (It always works for her.) We decide to bake dragon cookies and serve them for tea with my grandmother. That way, dragons will be on her mind when she talks with my parents about my birthday.

"Oh, lovely!" my grandmother says.

Rapunzel crosses her fingers at me.

"These fairy cookies are so pretty and so delicious," Grandmother continues. I sigh.

"I think my grandmother misplaced her glasses again," I whisper.

Oh well.

My father is my last resort. After Rapunzel leaves, I go into the study, where he is watching the royal news.

On TV, a reporter named Esther Rubinoff is talking about some problems with the environment. She mentions that the royal forests aren't as thick and green as they once were and the farmlands aren't growing as many fruits and vegetables anymore. Worst of all, some of the dragons seem to be losing their sparkle and ability to breathe fire—a sign that they are probably sick. This makes me so sad. Someone needs to help them.

That's it! I know how to show my parents I'm responsible enough to have a dragon. I'm going to investigate and figure out what the problem is! I run up to my room and start looking through the dragon books I checked out. Tomorrow I can go back to the library at school to do some more research, and I'll definitely need to put together a dragon kit to bring on the field trip. Luckily, my aunt Rachel promised to take Rapunzel and me to the Elves, Minstrels, and Fairies Bazaar in the afternoon. It will be the perfect place to find what I need.

~ ◎ Chapter 9 ◎ ~
My Very Own
Dragon Kit

As soon as I get to school, I tell Rapunzel about my plan. I'm so excited that the day flies by. When we get to the bazaar, I head straight for Magical Creatures Pet and Supply. Rapunzel ducks into a salon that promises, even if it can't make you *fairest of them all*, it can tame your unmanageable hair. I figure it will take them a little while to tame Rapunzel's hair, so I'll have plenty of time to collect everything I need for my dragon kit.

I've done my homework, and know exactly what to get:

Dragon Field Guide	✓
Binoculars	✓
Flashlight	✓
Rope	✓

. . . and a backpack to carry it all!

When I come out of the shop, I hear something.

"Psst. Emma!" A girl in a cape is trying to get my attention. "Emma!"

She knows my name!?

"Rapunzel, is that you?" I say, finally realizing. "Why are you being so mysterious and what are you doing under a cape?"

"Well," she says . . . and pushes back the cape. I just about drop all my packages.

"Oh, my, Rapunzel, you have very short and very pink hair!"

"I know," she says, and sighs.

Aunt Rachel and I take Rapunzel to Sweets, Treats, and Fairy Eats, our favorite

dessert shop, to cheer her up. Rapunzel and I share the fizzing ice-cream soda with rainbow POP ice-cream and two giant swirly straws. (Nobody can be sad eating a fizzing ice-cream soda!)

That night, at a family dinner, I tell my parents about my plan to figure out what's hurting the dragons and show them my dragon kit. My cousin Ben and his family are there too.

Ben teases, "So you haven't given up on the Royal Dragon Guard, huh, Emma?"

He doesn't mean to hurt my feelings, but he kind of does. I can tell he still thinks it's funny that I would want to fly dragons, even though I'm not five years old anymore. He thinks it's impossible that I'd ever truly be a dragon rider.

My father thinks that figuring out what's wrong with the dragons may be too much for a princess. My uncle Alan tells me that even the Royal Council hasn't been able to figure out what's causing the problem. When I tuck Lola and Harold in for the night, I'm still determined to try.

~ ◎ Chapter 10 ◎ ~
# The Dragon Caverns

Yay! It's time to board the carriages. I've got my notebook and my dragon kit, and I'm all ready. Rapunzel and I sit together. Everyone has noticed her hair, but Rapunzel is trying to make the best of it. I'm glad the field trip will help take her mind off it.

The carriages are pulling up at the

entrance to the caverns. The gnomes who are waiting for us sure look grumpy. I think they make even Lady Mary a little nervous. She clears her throat twice before reminding us of the rules for the field trip.

"Now girls, remember to stay with your partners. Pay close attention to our guides, and *don't* wander off in any of the cavern tunnels."

We set off. The tunnels twist and turn. Lanterns on the wall light the way, but it's pretty dark in some of the passageways.

Alex is right ahead of me. She whispers, "I would hate to be lost in here!"

"I know," I answer. But inside, I can't wait to see the dragons.

Our first stop is the hatchery. Even though dragon fire has singed some spots, I'm surprised to see how leafy the trees are and how lush the moss and ferns are here. The hatchery feels like a giant green pillow for dragon eggs. It turns out heat helps the eggs hatch. I make some notes and draw a picture of the hatchery in my dragon field guide.

As the gnomes lead us farther into the caverns, it starts to get cooler. You can barely see the rock ceilings, they're so far overhead. All of a sudden we come out into an open area surrounded by cliffs. I can see baby dragons peeking out of nests tucked into nooks. Bigger dragons fly overhead.

I wonder how Lola and Harold would get along with a baby dragon. Or how Mom and Dad would. I pull the binoculars out of my backpack to get a closer look. But when I look through them, I see something I didn't notice at first. The dragons actually look a little tired and faded—not bright and sparkly like they should.

I want to watch for longer, but the gnomes start to lead us back into another tunnel. By the time I put my binoculars away, my group—Rapunzel, Moriah, Alex, and I—is the last in line. "Come on!" Rapunzel says. "We need to keep up."

My mind is busy. How am I going to figure out what the problem is? I need some clues. I'm so deep in thought, I must have stopped without knowing, because Rapunzel bumps into me. Moriah stumbles into her. Alex crashes into all of us, and my back-pack flies off and bangs against the lantern on the wall.

CRASH!

We all freeze. I feel around for my back-pack and find the flashlight.

CLICK.

Everyone talks at the same time.

"Ouch!" I say.

"What happened?" Rapunzel asks.

Moriah says, "Why on earth were you running, Alex?!"

"How was I supposed to know you all were going to stop!" Alex says.

I can't help it—I start to laugh. We're a four-princess pile-up.

Rapunzel and Alex giggle. Pretty soon, we're all laughing.

"Uh-oh," says Moriah. She looks around. "Where *is* everybody?!"

The rest of our class is gone. They must

have turned in to one of the other tunnels. But which one?!

"What are we going to do?" Alex says.

No one answers.

"Um . . . I think we're going to have to find a gnome to ask for help."

All eyes turn to me. "Wait a second! I said 'we,' not me!"

"Come on, Emma," Alex says.

Even Moriah chimes in. "Please, Emma!"

I'm pretty nervous about the idea of talking to a strange gnome, but I choose one of the tunnels. Rapunzel, Alex, and Moriah follow close behind me. There's a not-so-happy-looking gnome coming toward us. I stop and take a deep breath.

"Excuse me, Mr. Gnome, sir, but we've lost our way."

He mutters something about "interfering Royal Council and underfoot princesses," and hurries past us. This is definitely *not* going to be easy.

~ ◎ Chapter 11 ◎ ~
A School for Gnomes

After a while, we come to a big stone building carved into the side of the rock. It has a sign that says *The Gnarly Gnome Preparatory School.*

"Well . . . I guess we'll find some gnomes to ask here," says Alex. But she looks like she's not too eager to go in.

"I bet this time it will be better," Rapunzel

says, but I can tell even she might not believe it.

"Or not," Moriah says, when she can't budge the door. We finally manage to pull it open, but it takes all of us. Whew!

The classes are in session, so we tiptoe. As I look around, I can't help wondering what it would be like to go to school here. There are

lots of carved statues of dragons and other magical creatures, large pieces of rock with amazing gems in them, and cases full of interesting-looking tools. There's also a big poster about dragon care that I wish I could stop and read. I almost knock over a stone statue because I'm so busy looking around. Moriah catches it just in time!

"Shhh—be careful!" she says. "We don't want to attract too much attention. Or we won't be going on any more field trips. *Ever*."

Good point.

BRRRINNG, clangs the bell. Class must be over.

We freeze. "Quick, in here!" I say, and pull open a door.

The good news is, it's a closet. The not so good news is, it's a little bit tight for four.

Okay, *very* tight.

Who knew that gnomes getting out of class sound like a herd of wild unicorns?! Or take so long!

When it's finally quiet again, I peek my head out. I see a gnome who looks like he's about our age, standing in front of a bulletin board—*alone*. I try to act braver than I feel.

It turns out his name is Justin, and he's

in his second year at Gnome Prep. I get the feeling he's not your typical gnome. He actually seems excited to meet some live princesses.

When I explain that we have to get back to our class, Justin suggests we walk into the main village to see if we can find a dragon that can fly us back to our class. He has his own pet dragon—lucky him! But she's not full-grown yet, so she isn't big enough to carry all of us.

I think this is a great plan! Moriah, Alex, and Rapunzel are not so happy about the "flying on a dragon" part.

~ ⊚ Chapter 12 ⊚ ~
Dragon to the Rescue

Justin takes us on a narrow path up a rocky hill. When we get to the top, we can see the whole village! Moriah gasps. Rapunzel beams. Alex's eyes get huge.

I open my mouth, but nothing comes out. Because there, in front of us, is a large lake surrounded by hundreds of homes—in all sorts of odd shapes and sizes, with statues and gardens all carved out of stone. The lake sparkles, and it almost looks like it's snowing because the gnomes are busy cutting, carving, or polishing stone, with glittery dust flying. It's like being in a giant snow globe.

There's only one thing missing from this perfect fairy tale picture.

"But where are the dragons?" I say.

Justin looks down. "The Royal Council is worried about them being near the cavern lakes, so now they're not allowed to fly free in this area."

"Why doesn't the Royal Council want them near the lakes?" Alex asks.

"Because the dragons used to swim in the lakes," Justin says. "The council was

worried that their fires would scorch the bank or make the waters too warm."

"So that's why we haven't seen any dragons in a while," I say.

"And why the gnome we saw earlier didn't want to talk to us—he was angry with the Royal Council," Moriah adds.

"Um, I hate to interrupt," Alex says, "but are we going to have to cross that bridge?"

"Yes," says Justin. "There's no other way to get from this hillside into the village."

Alex, Moriah, and I look at Rapunzel.

"What is it?" Justin asks.

"Rapunzel doesn't really like heights," I say.

"Too much time in towers," Moriah adds.

"Don't worry," says Rapunzel. "I just won't look down."

We start across. The glittery dust swirls in the breeze, and the bridge sways a little. Justin goes first, I follow, and Rapunzel comes next. Then Alex and Moriah. Rapunzel isn't looking down, which is good. Right up until the point when she trips. I try to catch her but wind up with an armful of cape.

"AHHHHHH!"

SPLASH!

I grab the rope out of my backpack. But it isn't long enough to reach the water! Justin pulls a whistle out of his pocket and blows three times. A dragon appears in the distance. She is coming toward us fast! I can see that Rapunzel is okay because her dress has billowed up and she's floating. But she's stuck because the lake is so big.

The dragon pulls up right next to the bridge, and Justin practically leaps onto her back.

"Come on," he says, looking at me. "I need both hands to steer close to the water. You'll have to grab your friend."

Me? Ride a dragon! My heart does a happy skip, even though I'm worried about

Rapunzel. With Justin steadying me, I climb
onto the dragon's back.

We soar up, up into the air. For a
moment, time seems to stop. The wind
blows my hair back, and my heart does
a loop de loop. I rub my hand against the
dragon's smooth scales. The sun glints off
her wings as she glides. It's the best feel-

ing in the world—just like I imagined! If Rapunzel weren't in trouble, I would want to fly for hours.

When we're close enough, the dragon dips and swoops low over the water, right above Rapunzel.

She dives even lower, and I stretch to reach Rapunzel. I'm not sure if the dragon will be able to carry our weight. I can hear Moriah and Alex yelling "Oh no!" and "Hold on!" in surprisingly un-princess-y tones. We sink, and skim the lake for a moment. Then we touch down on the ground, and Rapunzel rolls off into the grass. I want to fly back over the lake again, but instead I tumble after her.

I land in grass *and* a carpet of long, lush, thick, and sparkly pink hair.

"Rapunzel," I say, trying to unwind myself, "your hair grew back." (Even Rapunzel's hair doesn't grow this fast.)

Justin slides off the back of the dragon, who must be his pet Druscilla, just as Moriah and Alex come running toward us.

"And then some!" Moriah says.

Alex hands Rapunzel back her cape so she can dry off, and we all start helping Rapunzel coil up her hair.

Not only is Rapunzel's hair long, pink, and sparkly, even Druscilla seems to sparkle more where she got wet. I can feel my mind trying to put the pieces together.

"I think," I say slowly, "the Royal Council has made a mistake."

~ ◎ Chapter 13 ◎ ~
Putting the Pieces Together

"What do you mean?" says Alex.

I picture the different places we saw in the caverns. "The council thought the dragons would do too much damage to farms and forests in the kingdom. But look at the hatchery!"

"What about it?" says Rapunzel, wringing out her hair.

"Some areas are a bit burned, but the whole place is green and the trees and plants are growing like crazy," I say. "I don't think it's a coincidence."

"You mean it's the dragon's fire that actually makes the hatchery so green?" says Moriah.

"Yes!" I say. "I think the heat must somehow help things grow."

"Oh," says Justin, like he's starting to see where I'm going with this. "The Royal Council's rule actually *hurts* the farmlands, even though they meant to protect them."

"And I'm pretty sure I know what's hurting the dragons!" I say. "The council thought they were protecting the cavern lakes, but not letting the dragons swim there had some results they didn't imagine."

Justin is nodding now.

"Swimming in the lakes is actually good for the dragons. See how sparkly Druscilla looks now? I think the dragons are losing their sparkle and ability to breathe fire because they aren't allowed to swim in the lake water!"

"You're right!" says Justin.

I grin at him.

"Plus now that I think about it, the banks of the lake *were* actually greener, and there were more reeds and water lilies in the lake before, when the dragons used to swim there." He's so excited, he's practically jumping up and down.

"Yay—you did it, Emma! You figured it out," exclaims Rapunzel.

At the inn, Justin talks to the stable

master and borrows one of their largest dragons—one that makes Druscilla look dainty by comparison. He climbs into the saddle. Rapunzel, Alex, and Moriah get up, with some help. (Rapunzel plans to shut her eyes.) And I can't believe it—Justin is going to let *me* fly Druscilla.

"Ready?" Justin asks.

I nod. I'm excited but a little nervous.

"Don't worry. Druscilla will follow this dragon," he says. "Here we go."

His dragon soars up over the hills, higher and higher. Then it swoops down over the lake. I pull on the reins the way Justin

showed me, and Druscilla follows. The wind whooshes in our ears, and sun sparks off the glittery stone snow. It's the best roller coaster ride ever.

"WHEEEeeeeeeeeeeeeeeeeeee!"

It's over way too soon! Lady Mary is so relieved to see us that she alternates between smiling and scolding. Then I explain my theory about the dragons and Justin's part in our adventure, and everyone oohs and ahhs over Rapunzel's long, sparkly pink hair. The gnomes nod and pat Justin on the back, and Lady Mary thanks him.

Then the gnomes shake my hand.

"Gnomes and dragons actually need each other, just like princesses and dogs!" I announce. Everyone laughs.

Behind me, I hear a voice that sounds familiar. It's the reporter Esther Rubinoff.

It turns out she is visiting the caverns so she can talk to the gnomes. Once she hears what happened, she asks if she can take our picture and use it in her report.

Rapunzel, Alex, Moriah, Justin, and I pose next to Druscilla.

When it's time to say good-bye, everyone walks out to the carriages together, and this time the gnomes look a lot happier than when they greeted us. Justin waves as we ride off.

Later that evening, my father and I take Lola and Harold for a walk before bed.

After a few minutes, he says, "I was wrong about the dragon problem being too hard for you, Emma. I'm very proud of you."

I feel warm inside, but in a good way.

This is the perfect moment I've been waiting for.

"With my birthday coming up in a few days . . . well, I've been wanting to ask if you and Mother might be okay with another pet."

"Emma, how many dogs does one princess need?" my father says, laughing.

"Well, it's not exactly a dog I had in mind . . ."

He hasn't said no so far. Cross your fingers for me!

~ ◎ Chapter 14 ◎ ~
Birthday Surprises

When I get to the Academy on my birthday, I don't see any of my classmates in the courtyard, even though I'm not late today. Where are they all? I run up the stairs, and this time I don't pause to look out the tower windows. I open the door and hurry into the classroom.

"Surprise!" everyone yells.

Wow! Am I ever surprised!

"The class wanted to do something special for your birthday, Princess Emma," says Lady Mary.

Rapunzel, Alex, *and* Moriah step forward carrying a dragon cake!

Moriah grins. "I don't think a dragon

pet is for me, but now I understand why you want one."

I smile back.

"And there are some special guests here today," Lady Mary says.

That's when I notice Justin standing

next to a distinguished-looking gnome at the front of the room. It turns out that the older gnome is the headmaster of Gnome Prep. They've come to say thank you and also to talk with the headmistress of the Academy about setting up an exchange program between our two schools.

So I may actually get to see what it's

like to go to Gnome Prep. And—best of all—Justin has promised me more rides on Druscilla!

"There are some other guests here I think you'll be happy to see, Emma," says Lady Mary.

My royal father and mother give me a hug.

"Our birthday present to you is in the courtyard," my father says.

I run to the window. There, sparkling in the sun, is the perfect dragon for me! My friends all crowd over to the window to look. There's lots of oohing and ahhing—I can't stop beaming. Then, everyone sings happy birthday, and we have cake. It's definitely the best birthday ever!

On the way back from the carriage stop that day, Ben asks me a million questions about dragons and gnomes. And, I have to admit, it feels great.

On Monday, Lady Mary asks the whole class to write an inspiring letter to the princesses who will be starting school next year. Here's mine:

Dear First-Year Princesses,

Don't sit around waiting for your fairy godmother.

You can still be a princess and . . . climb the tower, swim the moat, race the prince, and fly the dragon yourself.

After all, it's up to us to write our OWN stories.

I believe in you.

Love,

Princess Emma

Dragon Rider

The end.